CRÊPES BY Suzette

DUTTON CHILDREN'S BOOKS

New York

MONICA
WELLINGTON

Pour les trois filles
Combeau: Caroline Valérie,
Laura Adrienne,
and Charlotte Gabrielle

With grateful acknowledgment and thanks to
Diane Combeau, Diane Giddis, Denis Johnston,
Lucia Monfried, Irene Vandervoort,
Laura Wellington, Lydia Wellington,
and Patricia Zybert

ABOUT THE ART

The pictures in this book are mixed-media collages made up of color
copies of photos taken by the author on numerous trips to Paris;
ephemera such as postcards, tickets, and wrappers collected by the
author; and artwork colored with markers and colored pencils, cut out
with scissors, and pasted onto paper painted with acrylics.

Copyright © 2004 by Monica Wellington
All rights reserved.
CIP Data is available.
Published in the United States 2004 by Dutton Children's Books,
a division of Penguin Young Readers Group
345 Hudson Street, New York, New York 10014
www.penguin.com
Designed by Irene Vandervoort   Manufactured in China   First Edition
ISBN 0-525-46934-6
1 3 5 7 9 10 8 6 4 2

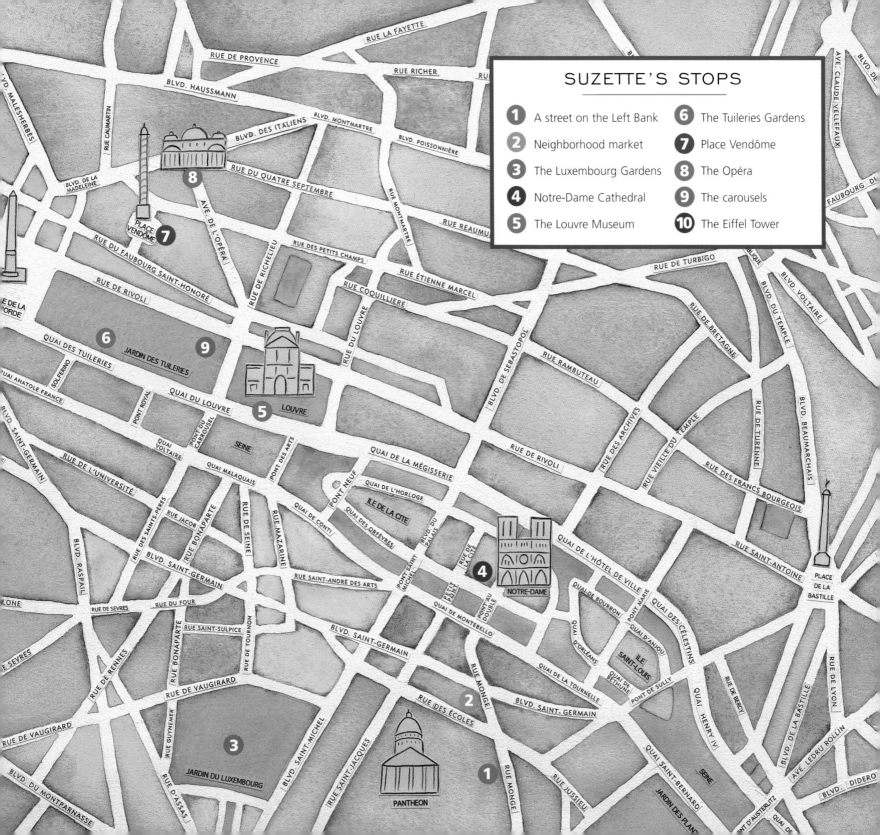

It is morning, and Suzette is mixing a big batch of batter. She is getting ready to make her special kind of pancakes, called *crêpes* in French. She cooks and sells them, ready to eat, from her street cart, which she takes all over the city of Paris.

SUCRE
CONFITURE
CITRON
CHOCOLAT
MIEL

Suzette's
CRÊPES

BANANE
POIRE
PÊCHE
POMME
FRAISE

Close to home, Suzette goes to her neighborhood market to choose the best fresh fruits for her *crêpes*. Finally her cart is loaded with everything she needs for the day. Now she is ready for customers.

On y va!

Suzette's friend the postman greets her, *Bonjour!* He stops for a chat and a morning treat. She will make him a tasty hot *crêpe* filled with fresh raspberries, his favorite. He is her first customer of the day.

Suzette pushes her cart into the park. The people sitting on the grass are happy to see her. She offers many different kinds of *crêpes*, and it is hard for them to choose. They decide on *crêpes* filled with fruit jams, *s'il vous plaît.*

SUCRE
CONFITURE
CITRON
CHOCOLAT
MIEL

Suzette's
CRÊPES

BANANE
POIRE
PÊCHE
POMME
FRAISE

BEURRE

A child has just fallen down, and his mother is comforting him. How about a *crêpe* with banana? *Oui.* Suzette pours the creamy batter onto her hot griddle and smooths it out into a thin, perfectly round pancake. The boy feels much better already.

As Suzette pushes her cart along the river, she meets street musicians filling the air with fast, jazzy sounds. They signal her over and call out what they want. Their first *crêpe* sizzles, and the edges turn crispy and golden.
Oh là là!

cannelle

SUCRE

BEURRE

SUCRE
CONFITURE
CITRON
CHOCOLAT
MIEL

Suzette's
CRÊPES

BANANE
POIRE
PÊCHE
POMME
FRAISE

Outside the museum,
an artist is working on
a portrait. He is ready to take
a break and wants a snack,
tout de suite. At just the
right moment, Suzette flips
the *crêpe* over with
her long spatula.

SUCRE

Cannelle

SUCRE
CONFITURE
CITRON
CHOCOLAT
MIEL

Suzette's
CRÊPES

BANANE
POIRE
PÊCHE
POMME
FRAISE

From the gardens close by come the laughter and chatter of children just dismissed from school. They all want *crêpes* filled with chocolate.

C'est bon!

SUCRE
CONFITURE
CITRON
CHOCOLAT
MIEL

Suzette's CRÊPES

BANANE
POIRE
PÊCHE
POMME
FRAISE

chocolat

A fancy lady out shopping craves something sweet. The mouth-watering smells rise up from the cart and tempt her. Suzette folds the *crêpe* neatly in half, then sprinkles it with sugar. *Voilà!*

SUCRE
CONFITURE
CITRON
CHOCOLAT
MIEL

Suzette's
CRÊPES

BANANE
POIRE
PÊCHE
POMME
FRAISE

SUC

BEURRE

A dancer is
on her way to the theater
for a rehearsal of tonight's
ballet performance.
Would she like a zesty lemon
crêpe to give her an
extra burst of energy?
Oui, bien sûr.

Suzette has many
customers by the carousels,
and she quickly cooks
one *crêpe* after another.
She spreads them with delicious
fillings and folds them into
triangles to hand out.
Vite, vite!

SUCRE
CONFITURE
CITRON
CHOCOLAT
MIEL

Suzette's
CRÊPES

BANANE
POIRE
PÊCHE
POMME
FRAISE

Suzette makes a *crêpe*
for her last customers,
the honeymooners, to share.
She hands it to them, wrapped
in paper, warm and sweet.
They thank her together.
Merci beaucoup.

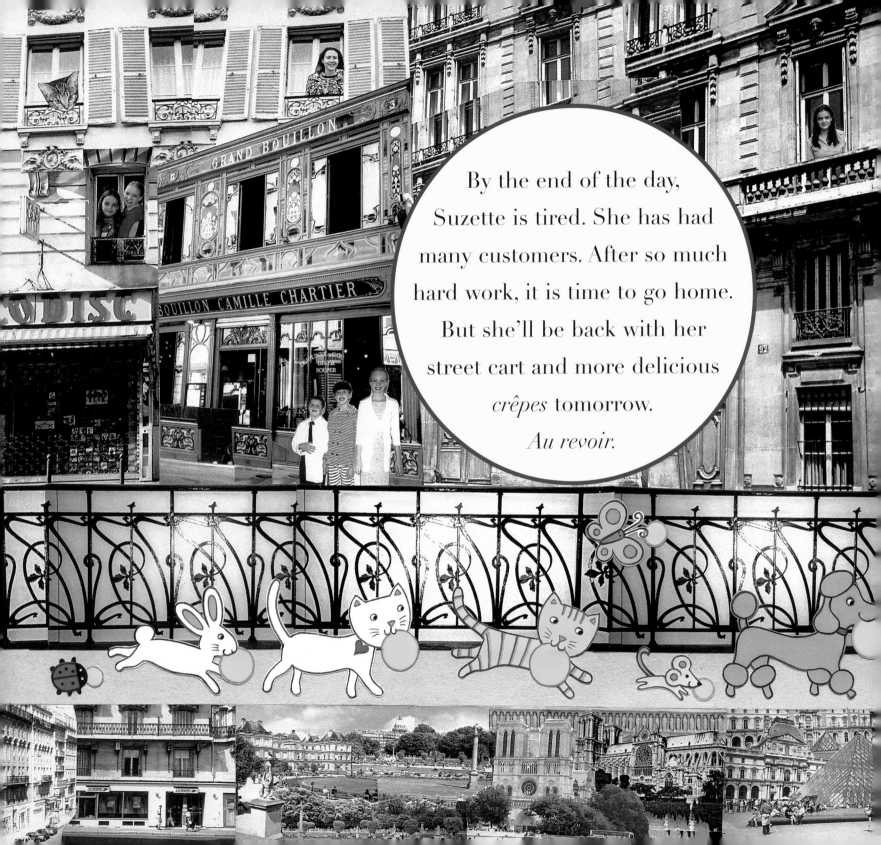

By the end of the day, Suzette is tired. She has had many customers. After so much hard work, it is time to go home. But she'll be back with her street cart and more delicious *crêpes* tomorrow.

Au revoir.

SUCRE
CONFITURE
CITRON
CHOCOLAT
MIEL

Suzette's
CRÊPES

BANANE
POIRE
PÊCHE
POMME
FRAISE

Suzette's
CRÊPE RECIPE

(Makes about 8 crêpes)

2 eggs	1 tablespoon melted butter
1 cup milk	1 tablespoon sugar
1 cup flour	1/4 teaspoon salt

UTENSILS: a big bowl, whisk, ladle, spatula, and a large frying pan

In the bowl, beat the eggs with a whisk. Beat in the milk. Then add the flour and mix well until very smooth. Add the melted butter, sugar, and salt to the batter and blend well. It should be the consistency of very heavy cream. Add slightly more milk if necessary. (Alternatively, the mixing can be done in a blender or food processor.) The batter can be used immediately, but even better, cover and chill 1 hour or overnight.

Heat the pan and brush lightly with melted butter. Pour in a ladleful of batter (about 3 tablespoons). Quickly swirl the pan around so the batter spreads out thin. Cook over medium-high heat until the crêpe is set and the edges are lightly browned and lift up easily, about 2 minutes. Flip it, spread it with your favorite filling, and cook for about another minute. Fold it in half, and then in half again, creating a triangle, then serve!

Bon appétit!

THE POSTMAN
Based on portraits by Vincent van Gogh (1853–1890) of the postman Joseph Roulin, 1888–89; versions at the Museum of Modern Art, New York; Museum of Fine Arts, Boston; and elsewhere.

ON THE GRASS
Based on *Luncheon on the Grass,* 1862–63, by Édouard Manet (1832–1883); versions at Musée d'Orsay, Paris, and Courtauld Institute Galleries, London.

MOTHER AND CHILD
Based on *The Bath,* c.1891, by Mary Cassatt (1884–1926); at the Art Institute of Chicago.

THE STREET MUSICIANS
Based on *Three Musicians,* 1921, by Pablo Picasso (1881–1973); at the Museum of Modern Art, New York.

THE ARTIST
Portrait based on *Mona L[isa]* 1503–6, by Leonardo da Vinci (1452–1519); at the Louvre, Paris.

GLOSSARY OF FRENCH WORDS USED IN THIS BOOK

abricot	apricot
au revoir	good-bye
banane	banana
beurre	butter
bien sûr	of course
bon appétit	enjoy your meal
bonjour	hello
cannelle	cinnamon
c'est bon	it's good
chocolat	chocolate
citron	lemon
confiture	jam
crêpe	thin pancake
farine	flour
fraise	strawberry
framboise	raspberry
lait	milk
merci beaucoup	thank you very much
miel	honey
oeuf	egg
oh là là!	wow!
on y va	let's go
oui	yes
pêche	peach
poire	pear
pomme	apple
prune	plum
sel	salt
s'il vous plaît	please
sucre	sugar
tout de suite	right away
vite	quick
voilà!	there!

NOTES ON THE PICTURES

The scenes in the pictures are based on real places in Paris. Suzette's customers are based on figures from famous paintings and sculptures by French artists or by artists who lived and worked in France (identified at the bottom of these pages).

COPYRIGHT & DEDICATION This is a rendition of a map of the city of Paris with major street names and famous landmarks identified.

IN THE MORNING This scene takes place on a typical Parisian street. These particular buildings are mostly on rue Monge on the Left Bank.

THE OUTDOOR MARKET Every district in Paris has outdoor street markets. This one is made up of photos taken at various neighborhood markets.

THE POSTMAN This scene is a mixture of streets close to the Luxembourg Gardens.

ON THE GRASS This scene takes place in the Luxembourg Gardens.

MOTHER AND CHILD This scene also takes place in the Luxembourg Gardens.

THE STREET MUSICIANS This scene takes place along the River Seine looking across to Île de la Cité and Notre-Dame Cathedral.

THE ARTIST This scene takes place by the Louvre Museum with the glass pyramids by I. M. Pei in front.

SCHOOLCHILDREN This scene takes place in the Tuileries Gardens by the Louvre.

THE SHOPPER This scene takes place by the Place Vendôme.

THE DANCER This scene takes place by the Opéra, Paris's famed opera house, also called the Palais-Garnier.

THE CAROUSELS This scene is a mixture of various carousels in Paris, especially in the Tuileries Gardens.

THE HONEYMOONERS This scene takes place in the gardens surrounding the Eiffel Tower.

END OF THE DAY This scene is a mixture of various buildings, mostly on the Left Bank. At the bottom, in the border, is a view of each of the places Suzette has been during her day in Paris.

SCHOOLCHILDREN
Based on *Dance,* 1909, by Henri Matisse (1869–1954); at the Museum of Modern Art, New York.

THE SHOPPER
Based on a poster, *La revue blanche,* 1895, by Henri de Toulouse-Lautrec (1864–1901); at Musée Toulouse-Lautrec, Albi, France.

THE DANCER
Based on the sculpture *The Little Fourteen-Year-Old Dancer,* 1880–81, by Edgar Degas (1834–1917); versions at the Metropolitan Museum of Art, New York; Tate Gallery, London; Musée d'Orsay, Paris; and elsewhere.

THE CAROUSELS
Performers based on *The Circus,* 1891, by Georges Seurat (1859–1891); at Musée d'Orsay, Paris.

THE HONEYMOONERS
Based on *The Bride and Groom of the Eiffel Tower,* 1938–1939, by Marc Chagall (1887–1985); Musée National d'Art Moderne; Centre Georges Pompidou, Paris.

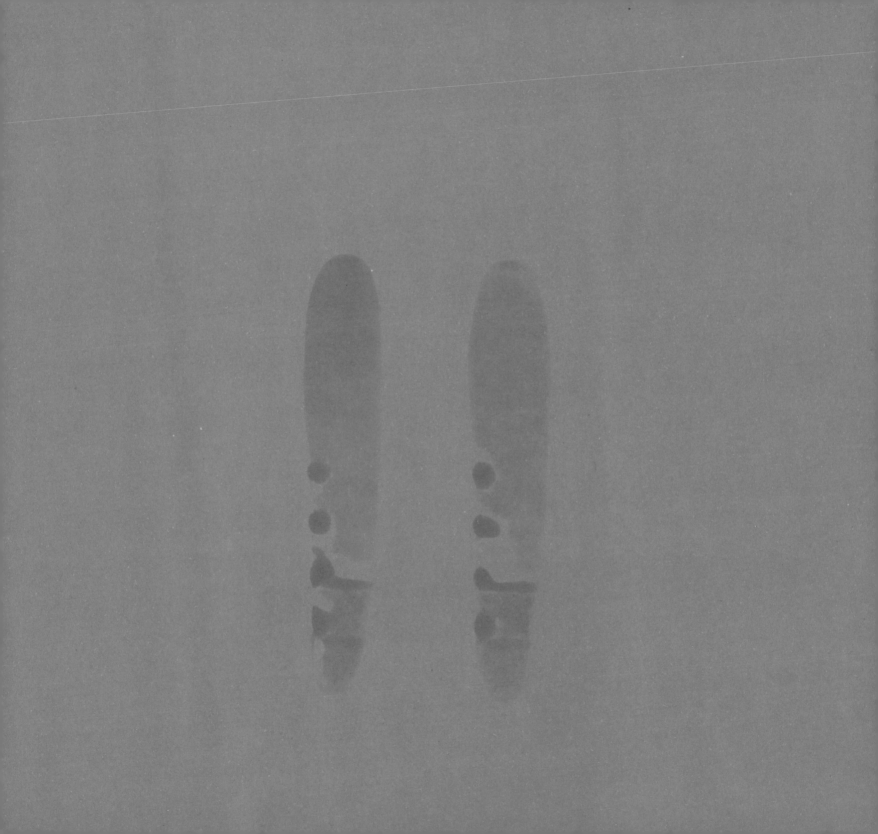

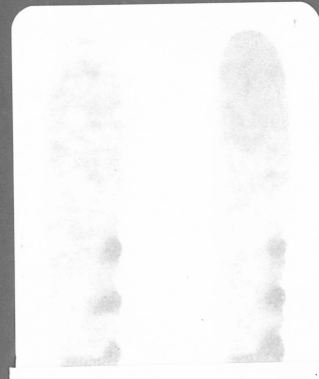